Monkey

All rights reserved. No part of this publication may be
reproduced, without the prior permission of the copyright owner.

The views and ideas expressed in this book are the personal opinions of the author, and do not necessarily
represent the views of the Publisher.

© Copyright 2022 by Perigee Trade

perigeetrade@proton.me

This is the story of the havoc created in Heaven by the Monkey King, which led to his imprisonment in a mountain.

After 500 years he was released to guard the monk Tripitaka on a journey to the West in quest of the holy Buddhist scriptures.

One day when the Monkey King was drilling the younger monkeys of Flower and Fruit Mountain in martial skills, he became dissatisfied with the strength of his sword.

'Why don't you go to the Dragon King at the bottom of the sea, Great Lord, and ask him for a better sword?' suggested an old monkey.

The Dragon King at the bottom of the sea produced a range of weapons for the Monkey King's approval.

'All too light!' pronounced Monkey. 'Haven't you anything stronger than these?'

At last the Dragon King produced a special treasure: the as-you-wish magic staff made of pearly iron which was used for stilling the rivers and seas. It weighed more than 6000 kilos.

Monkey seized it enthusiastically.
'That's far too powerful for you!' piped the Dragon King.

But arrogant Monkey reduced the as-you-wish staff to the size of a personal cudgel and skipped off with it.

The Dragon King reported Monkey's audacity to the Celestial Emperor in Heaven. 'Get him up here where we can keep an eye on him. Give him some minor position,' suggested the God of Venus.

'Good idea!' The Celestial Emperor decreed that Monkey would become the Master of the Imperial Stables, the lowest-ranking position in Heaven.

The God of Venus was sent to fetch him.

Flattered and unsuspecting, Monkey accepted the promotion. He chose his own route to Heaven on a magic cloud. Showing off, he performed one of his famous somersaults, covering 68,000 kilometres.

As Master of the Imperial Stables, Monkey soon rebelled. He felt sorry for the imperial steeds, forever tethered in the clouds. So he set them free.

And when he discovered that his post was below all others in Heaven, he tore off his Imperial Studmaster's red cloak and overturned the Imperial Studmaster's desk.

'I don't have to take a piddling post in Heaven! I'd rather be home on Flower and Fruit Mountain!' he shouted.

'I resign!'

The Celestial Emperor was angry; he ordered a heavenly guard, under the command of Heavenly King Li, to arrest the insolent Monkey.

Wielding his magic staff, Monkey defeated his assailants, one by one. He felt insuperable.

'Tell the Celestial Emperor,' he declared, 'that my new name is Great Holy One: Equal of Heaven.'

At his wit's end, the Celestial Emperor decreed that Monkey could keep the empty title of 'Great Holy One', if that would keep him under control.

'You're to be in charge of Grandma Wang's Divine Peach Orchard, Great Holy One,' grovelled the local god of land who was sent to give the news.

Then came Nezha, the baby-faced prince with three heads and three pairs of arms, brandishing a spear and waving magic rings.

'Good try!' shouted Monkey; and sent the ferocious Nezha packing.

'The peach trees are personally tended by Grandma Wang and can only be eaten at Grandma Wang's Peach Banquet. Those who eat the divine peaches live forever and never grow old.'

The new Keeper of the Peach Orchard set himself up among the ripest of his charges – and began eating. 'Sweet! Juicy! Delicious!'

Monkey had a peach feast every day. After eating his fill, he would transform himself into a tiny figure only a few centimetres high, and sink into sleep.

Grandma Wang was to hold a banquet for important dignitaries. She sent her fairy maidens to fetch some peaches of immortality, instructing them to report first to the Great Holy One.

At last they found Monkey reduced to a miniature of himself and basking among the leaves.

'Who's been invited to this feast?' he demanded. 'Am I on the list?'

When the fairies hung their heads, too embarrassed to confess the truth, he suspended them in air so they couldn't move.
Then he returned himself to his full size and hurried to the Yao Zhi Palace, where the banquet was to be held.

The banquet was laid out ready. The guests had not yet arrived. The fragrant smell of wine and food was too much for Monkey. He plucked a few hairs from his body and shouted 'Change!' The hairs were transformed into tiny sleep-bringing insects which buzzed around the guards and sent them to sleep.

Monkey ate and drank all he could, then crammed the rest into his cosmic bag, for the other monkeys on Flower and Fruit Mountain.

On the way home, drowsy with food and wine, he blundered into the Dou Sai Palace, home of the Supreme Taoist Dignitary...

... and found, beside the stove, several gourds containing golden pills of immortality. Monkey consumed all the pills in one swig.

'Now I'll be in trouble!' he groaned, unrepentant. Then he somersaulted off home to Flower and Fruit Mountain to host a giant monkey feast.

The Celestial Emperor, infuriated, ordered the four Heavenly Kings and an army of 10,000 troops to arrest Monkey, by any means. Magic weapons were brought in to subdue him. First a huge umbrella, a special monkey trap, and then a magic lute, the sound of which made the other monkeys feel weak.

The Celestial Emperor had been receiving a string of complaints about Monkey. Grandma Wang had reported the theft of the peaches of immortality and the disruption of her Divine Banquet. The Supreme Taoist Dignitary had reported the disappearance of his golden pills.

'I've had enough of this!'

Monkey pierced a hole in the canopy of the umbrella and rescued all his monkey forces. Then he removed the magic weapons from the hands of his assailants with his own magic – and the attackers ran away.

The god Erlang, a superb fighter, was the next adversary. Erlang's double-edged, triple-pointed magic sword was no match for an as-you-wish magic staff.

Monkey confidently raised his pearly iron cudgel – but Erlang's ferocious dog leapt forward with bared teeth to snap at the defender's unprotected heels.

To dodge Erlang's double-edged triple-pointed sword, Monkey changed himself into a tiny bird.

Next, Monkey camouflaged himself as a small fish, and leapt into a mountain stream.

Erland immediately took the shape of a strong-beaked gobbler of little birds.

Erlang camouflaged himself as a fish eagle, gobbler of little fish.

Erlang was unstoppable.

Monkey was not done yet. He bravely fought on.

In desperation, to escape the notice of Erlang, Monkey took the form of a temple.

Realising that his tail was still showing, he quickly turned it into a flagpole erected at the back of the temple.

'Po!' scoffed Erlang. And the temple disappeared.

By now the battle had moved to the gates of the Dou Sai Palace of the Supreme Taoist Dignitary. Seeing the Great Holy One outside, surrounded by battling gods, the Supreme Taoist Dignitary threw a magic steel bracelet at his insolent head – and encircled him with it.

The Celestial Emperor decreed that Monkey be put on the platform of execution and put to death.

The celestial executioners tried hacking with swords, chopping with axes, striking with thunder and burning with fire, but they could not destroy the Great Holy One, because he had eaten so many divine peaches and immortality pills.

Eventually the Celestial Emperor ordered that Monkey be placed in the stove of the eight divine symbols and reduced to ashes.

After seven weeks, the cauldron was opened.

Monkey leapt out unharmed; and knocked over the Supreme Taoist Dignitary, who was standing gloating in his path.

Monkey felt all-powerful, indestructible, invincible.

'I can transform myself into seventy-two shapes,' he boasted. 'I can cover 68,000 kilometres in one somersault. I am in charge of the clouds.'

The Celestial Emperor was at the end of his tether. He appealed to Buddha Ru Lai from the West, ruler of clouds and mist, to subdue the Monkey 'Holy One'.

Buddha Ru Lai answered the Celestial Emperor's call. 'If you can somersault out of my right palm,' the Buddha told Monkey, 'I will appoint you to the position of Celestial Emperor.'

'Out of your right palm?' repeated Monkey. 'Simple!'

He did a magnificent somersault, one of his best. In mid-flight he passed five flesh-red pillars. As he flashed past, he wrote on the pillars: 'The Great Holy One was here!'

He turned around to make another somersault – and found he was still in the Buddha's hand!

Monkey was confused. He must have gone further than the end of the Buddha's hand! He was just about to prove that he was right – he had written on the flesh-red pillars, they couldn't be just fingers of the Buddha's hand! – when he was catapulted out of Heaven by the Buddha, and pressed into the mountain of Wu Hong, where he remained for the next 500 years.

He was at last released to guard the monk Tripitaka on his journey to the West in quest of the Buddhist holy scriptures.

On that journey, the Monkey King rid the world of many evil spirits and performed many good deeds.